The **MAD**®

Student Survival Guide
for Those Bored of Education

D1057425

The MAD
Student Survival Guide
for Those Bored of Education
By "The Usual Gang of Idiots"

SCHOLASTIC INC.

New York   Toronto   London   Auckland   Sydney
Mexico City   New Delhi   Hong Kong   Buenos Aires

If you purchased this book without a cover, you should be aware that this book is stolen property. It was reported as "unsold and destroyed" to the publisher, and neither the author nor the publisher has received any payment for this "stripped book."

No part of this publication may be reproduced in whole or in part, or stored in a retrieval system, or transmitted in any form or by any means, electronic, mechanical, photocopying, recording, or otherwise, without written permission of the publisher. For information regarding permission, write to E.C. Publications, Inc., 1700 Broadway, New York, NY 10019.

ISBN 0-439-38201-7

© 2002 by E.C. Publications, Inc. All rights reserved.

MAD, boy's head device, and all related indicia are trademarks of E.C. Publications, Inc.

Cover art by Norman Mingo.
Back cover art by Bob Clarke.
Cover design by Bethany Dixon.

All rights reserved. Published by Scholastic Inc., 557 Broadway, New York, NY 10012.
SCHOLASTIC and associated logos are trademarks and/or registered trademarks of Scholastic Inc.

12 11 10 9 8 7 6 5 4 3 2   2 3 4 5 6 7/0

Printed in the U.S.A.
First Scholastic printing, April 2002   40

Contents

THE MAD STUDENTS
HATE BOOK

ARTIST: AL JAFFEE   WRITERS: AL JAFFEE AND JODY REVENSON   IDEA BY: MIKE CLAUSSEN

DON'T YOU HATE…

…being the only one in Home Economics who misread the recipe.

DON'T YOU HATE…

…when the teachers in your school are
the only ones who refuse to go on strike.

DON'T YOU HATE…

…when your teacher suggests the topics for term reports and
there isn't one single subject that doesn't make you nauseous.

DON'T YOU HATE...

...finding out that the kid you copied those test answers from is even dumber than you are.

DON'T YOU HATE...

...having study hall when all your friends have classes.

...having classes when all your friends have study hall.

DON'T YOU HATE...

...having a teacher with bad breath who constantly looks over your shoulder.

DON'T YOU HATE...

...being the only one in class who isn't wearing designer jeans.

DON'T YOU HATE...

...wobbly study hall or library tables.

DON'T YOU HATE...

...sneezing in class and not having a hanky or tissue.

DON'T YOU HATE...

HOMEWORK FOR EASTER
READ CHAPTERS
4 THROUGH 96
WRITE 500 WORD
ESSAY ON EACH
CHAPTER

...teachers who assign homework over vacation breaks.

DON'T YOU HATE...

Ribbit

...biology class practical jokers.

DON'T YOU HATE...

...being the smartest one in the class.

DON'T YOU HATE...

...being the only one in Math class without a calculator.

DON'T YOU HATE...

...bumping into the teacher whose class you just cut.

DON'T YOU HATE...

...having a locker next to the smelliest kid in school.

TORTURE OF LEARNING DEPT.

Although parents are aware that taxes get higher every year to pay for well-equipped schools, kids are equally aware that the quality of school equipment gets lower every year. This doesn't seem plausible, except to those who've browsed through a devilish catalogue that was recently delivered to the *MAD* office by mistake. It reveals a couple of interesting things about some members of local school boards: (1) They enjoy pocketing a fast buck; (2) They also enjoy grinding spirited children down into docile, obedient nervous wrecks. Sad to say, there's a mail-order firm that happily serves this crowd by replacing education's three R's with its own three S's: Shoddiness, Skulduggery and Stupidity. Chances are, you'd probably never learn about this monstrous company unless you stumbled across its secret catalogue, as we did. And since that's not likely to happen accidentally, we'll just show you our copy on purpose, right here and now.

SCHOOL SUPPLIES UNLIMITED
WHOLESALE CATALOGUE

CROOKED TOOTH SAW

PAINFUL PAPER TOWELS

More Inside!

"TIP-EASY" SCHOOL CHAIRS

DELUXE TWO-SPEED DRINKING FOUNTAIN

FOR SCHOOL ADMINISTRATORS ONLY
SALES TO PARENTS, CHILDREN OR OTHER RADICALS IS PROHIBITED

ARTIST: BOB CLARKE WRITER: TOM KOCH

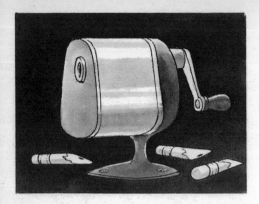

LOPSIDED BLADE ACTION lets this deluxe classroom sharpener chew up entire pencils without ever producing a usable point. A real money maker for school systems that sell pencils to students at a whopping mark-up over cost. Loud grinding noise is also good for disrupting studies.
23354—"LONG, HARD GRIND" BRAND SHARPENER..$4.98

"QUICK CHANGE" COMBINATION LOCK assures punishable tardiness when installed on student lockers. New improved model looks like an ordinary lock. But miraculously, the same combination never works twice to open it. Kids eventually give up hope, allowing school janitors to collect valuable personal belongings when they open locks with hack saws during summer vacation.
77351—"LOCK NESS MONSTER" BRAND LOCKS........$14.50 doz.

"SONGS AMERICAN CHILDREN HATE." This amazing book includes the hundred least-loved ballads of today's grade schoolers. Features all verses of such draggy numbers as "Flow Gently, Sweet Afton" and "Beautiful Dreamer." Guaranteed to turn kids away from music for life, and encourage them to devote full attention to the more profitable fine arts, such as computer programming.
8853—"OLDIES BUT BADDIES" SONG BOOK $5.95

ROLL DOWN-SNAP UP WALL MAP enables teachers to win the undivided attention of young daydreamers. Hair trigger roller mechanism recoils with a startling racket at the slightest touch of instructor's pointer. Maps of all continents available except Australia, which is too small to make enough noise.
19005—ATTENTION GETTER WALL MAPS......................$14.50 ea.

VISITING THE SCHOOL NURSE BE-COMES A MEMORABLE EXPERI-ENCE, once you equip her office with a prominent display of our frightening veterinary hypodermic needles. Watch young malingerers and hypochondriacs recover quickly, assuming your staff never tells them that the needles are really designed for tranquilizing elephants.
91117—SURE CURE HYPODER-MICS ....$2.60 ea.

DEFECTIVE M. & M. BRAND CRAYONS melt in your mouth and in your hand. Use of too much paraffin and watery dye in manufacturing this batch makes crayons become gooey soft when exposed to temperatures above 35 degrees. A double horror for kids as they get yelled at by teachers for ruining their artwork, and then get yelled at by parents for ruining their clothes.
5569—VIVID COLOR-LIVID REACTION CRAYONS.......................43¢ box

SILENCE ANNOYING SQUEALS OF EX-CITEMENT in your schoolyard during recess by providing children with one of our defective, deflated playground balls. Squeal-provoking games are utterly impossible with these lifeless babies, forcing kids to schloomp around in blessed, sullen silence. Order several. You'll be pleased with the results.
11528—DEAD, SQUOOSHY PLAY-GROUND BALL...........$1.75 ea.

DELUXE TWO-SPEED DRINKING FOUN-TAIN is specially designed for educational purposes. Secret setting can be changed in a jiffy from "Feeble Drip" to "Soaking Splash." Helps gullible primary graders learn never to take anything for granted in life. Also helps teach desert survival techniques by forcing kids to go through entire school day without drinkable water.
2791—DRENCH-OR-DRIBBLE DRINK-ING FOUNTAIN................$129.95

SCARY CLASSROOM ANIMALS enable youngsters to learn the meaning of fear while they're also learning the meaning of zoology. Why settle for insipid hamsters or white mice when iguanas and boa constrictors are hardier species better able to take care of themselves over weekends and vacations?

8842—VICIOUS BEASTS (ASSORTED TYPES AND SIZES)
$15 ea.

CHINTZY, ILL-FITTING COSTUMES can add a note of comedy to otherwise boring school pageants. We found these at a rummage sale and pass the savings on to you. Costumes feature cheap material, poor sewing and inaccurately marked sizes to assure you that kids will make fools of themselves on stage, and turn your next dull pageant into a laugh riot.

877—LOUSY LINCOLN COSTUME $6.65
878—PUNK PILGRIM COSTUME ..$6.85
879—CRUDDY XMAS COSTUME ..$7.29

MADDENING COPY MACHINE lowers student grade averages by cleverly smudging key words in quiz questions. Mechanism is equipped with irregular ink dribbler, automatic stencil ripper, cockeyed paper feeder and other illegibility devices not normally found on copiers in this price range.

26465—SMUDGY COPIER..........$47.50

CLEVERLY REARRANGED CLASSROOM NUMBERS can induce panicky confusion among even your coolest upperclassmen. We offer complete sets of handsome brass numerals, together with instructions for switching them around on your doors in a zany new sequence each semester. A great way to increase absenteeism in crowded schools by preventing students from finding their assigned classes.

33917—CLASSY BRASSY CLASSROOM NUMBERS..................$42 per 10

PRECISION WEATHER INSTRUMENT WITH ELECTRIC BELL ATTACHMENT automatically sounds alarm for school fire drill whenever temperature drops to zero or wind reaches 40 M.P.H. Completely eliminates risk of staging drills on nice warm days when children might actually enjoy going outdoors.

5578—CLANG-A-MATIC, PNEUMO-NIA-MATIC FIRE DRILL TIMER $49.95

INFERIOR SHOP TOOLS doom junior high school woodworking projects to botched up disaster from the word go. Helps youngsters learn to accept the agony of defeat as they struggle in vain to make bookends, etc. Tool defects are scarcely noticeable, causing kids to accept teacher's judgment that their own klutziness is responsible for lousy results.

33014—CROOKED TOOTH SAW..$8.50
33015—NICKED BLADE PLANE ..$7.75

WEIRDLY MARKED LAB EQUIPMENT helps turn even the simplest chemistry experiment into a student's nightmare. These test tubes were picked up cheap in a small European country that still uses such quaint measurements as hogsheads, gills and pennyweights. Impossibility of translating lab results into commonly used terms enables teachers to base final grades on pure whim.

6877—ODDBALL TEST TUBES ..26¢ ea.

OUT-OF-FOCUS SLIDE PROJECTOR makes all pictures look alike, thereby ending wasteful expense of buying new slides for new lectures. Poor lens quality coupled with non-functioning focus dial permit you to identify shapeless blobs on screen as anything you wish. Comes complete with "Scenic Italy" slide set for illustrating talks on biology, safe driving or even scenic Italy.

11519—G.A.F. (GOOD AND FUZZY) BRAND PROJECTOR........$79.75

"TIP-EASY" SCHOOL CHAIRS fool everyone with their deceptively sturdy appearance. Actually, each is handcrafted with a delicate center of balance that can be thrown out of whack with the slightest nudge. You'll want to fill your classrooms with plenty of these beauties to provide shy and clumsy students with a never ending source of embarrassment.

9055—NON-FOLDING CHAIRS THAT FOLD UP ANYWAY $32.50 ea.

FACTORY REJECT CHALK can be one of your teachers' best weapons in the fight to shatter youthful nerves. Soft texture contains just enough hard chalk lumps to assure one horrifying screech on blackboard before each stick breaks into numerous small pieces. Enjoy watching kids suffer from terrible noise, and then chew them out for wasting chalk.

29551—CRUMMY, CRUMBLY CHALK ....$3.50 doz. boxes

OUT-OF-DATE WORLD GLOBES serve the dual purpose of saving you money while they're making it impossible for your students to pass Geography. Also nice for young nostalgia buffs who prefer to learn about the world as it used to be. These globes are free of defects, and were imported by us from one of the finest map making firms in the Ottoman Empire.

28559—"OLD WORLD" BRAND SCHOOL GLOBES ..$8.50 ea.

BOTTLED LOCKER ROOM STENCH gives your gym facilities that "lived in" smell. Ideal for newly constructed schools where locker rooms have not yet become sufficiently gamy to make kids throw up when they're required to take Phys. Ed. right after lunch. Also great for confirming the younger generation's expressed belief that the whole world stinks.

11527—ESSENCE OF SWEAT SOCKS ..$2.75 per 6 oz. can

ENCOURAGE PAPER TOWEL CON-SERVATION in school rest rooms by filling dispensers with our Rough-'N-Ready brand toweling. Cheaply made from semi-raw wood pulp, leaving plenty of splinters and bark particles to dig into tender young skin. You save money as children quickly learn to let hands remain wet, or bring extra handkerchiefs from home.
**81442—PAINFUL PAPER TOWELS
29¢ pkg.**

WHY DEPEND ON SURPRISE QUIZZES to shatter children's nerves when flickering fluorescent lights in your classrooms can do the job more efficiently? Teachers will love the results as they watch our shoddy fixtures work sub-consciously to turn normally active kids into docile basket cases. Stock up on these factory rejects at special bargain prices.
**90268—FAULTY FLICKERING FLU-ORESCENT FIXTURES
$8.75 doz.**

GENUINE ALGAE SLIME-AND-GLYCERINE FLOOR POLISH creates an amazing slick surface that prevents boisterous youngsters from running in school hallways. Also prevents less boisterous youngsters from walking in school hallways. Order several cans to polish up your crummy floors while you polish off your crummy students.
4846—UPSY-DAISY FLOOR POL-ISH ....$3.50 gallon

2 EASY WAYS TO ORDER!

1) Visit us online at *inferiorschoolproducts.com*! You'll save .25 percent on all shipping charges and it will take you only a few hours to navigate our easy-to-use website!! Plus, we'll send you e-mails filled with special offers for as long as you live! (Sometimes 20 or 30 of them a week!)

2) Give us a call, toll-free (rotary phone users only). Remember, your call is very important to us, which is why we play Muzak while we keep you on hold as a recorded voice reminds you that your call is very important to us!

Public Schools are facing severe financial crises. Budgets are being cut, leaving students with old textbooks, faulty gym equipment and the like. What is the answer? Hit up big corporations for donations and sponsorship. Now, we can tolerate a new basketball scoreboard with a company's name on it, but a textbook that teaches math by having students count Tic Tacs is a whole other story. Can you say hidden agenda? Recently, we traveled to Pepsi High School in Long Beach, California, to find out what happens...

WHEN CORPORATE SPONSORSHIP OF PUBLIC SCHOOLS GOES TOO FAR!

From THE HOME DEPOT's

CHAPTER SIX: EXTINCTION

Extinction is a natural, necessary part of the Life Cycle. It is the process in nature by which, according to Darwin's Theory of Evolution, only the organisms best adapted to their environment tend to survive while those less adapted tend to be eliminated. In other words, every so often, bigger, stronger animals will enter an ecosystem and overwhelm the smaller animals that don't have the means to support themselves in the new, more competitive environment. As a result, the more efficient organisms take over and eventually, no one even remembers the extinct species. This is also referred to as *Natural Selection*.

66

2+2=4*

*"4" is the correct answer if reached during the initial grace period. Following the initial grace period, the sum shall be subject to an annual percentage rate of 17.99%, which corresponds to a daily periodic rate of 0.0493%. This rate will begin to accrue from the date the equation is assigned for homework and continue to accrue until the correct answer is credited to your midterms or final exams, whichever occurs first. If 30 days pass and the teacher has not received a minimum required answer, an additional late fee of 29 shall be added to the sum of the equation. So, if Johnny is given this equation in January and does not answer until February, the correct answer to "2+2" shall be calculated as 4+4X1.499%, or 4.05996,with a minimum required answer of 1. If Johnny does then not make the correct or minimum required answer until March, the correct answer to "2+2" shall be calculated as 4+4.05996X1.499%+29, or 33.12082, with a new minimum required answer of 2. (At current percentage rates, if only the minimum required answer is made each month, it will take 39 years to reach the correct answer. If Johnny is left back, he will be subject to a $25 annual membership fee.)

Life Sciences Book

Some Extinct Organisms:

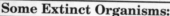

Wooly Mammoth

Saber-Toothed Tiger

Dodo Bird

Mom and Pop Small Corner Hardware Store

ARTIST: GEORGE WOODBRIDGE   WRITER: RICKY SPRAGUE

The Lighter Side of... School
(Part One)

ARTIST AND WRITER: DAVE BERG

22

A COLLECTION OF 9 MAD EXCUSES
THAT TEACHERS JUST MIGHT BUY
WHEN THEY ASK...

WHY DIDN'T YOU DO YOUR HOME-WORK?

ARTIST: PAUL COKER   WRITER: JOHN FICARRA

Your father used the last piece of looseleaf in the house as a "pooper scooper" when he walked the dog!

The battery in your pocket calculator went dead, and all the stores were closed!

You dozed off while meditating, and the next thing you knew, it was morning!

Your analyst was called away on an emergency, and you had to wait in his office the whole evening!

The air pollution was so bad that your eyes kept tearing, and you couldn't read a thing!

Last night was the concluding episode of a 22-part Educational TV Series, and you saw the first 21 parts!

You were taking karate lessons so you can ride in the subways again!

You went into one of those "24-hour Banking Centers," and wound up getting locked in the place all night.

You look upon home-work as an intrusion upon your "space"!

SNAPPY ANSWERS TO
HANS BRICKFACE

TUPID QUESTIONS AT
MEMORIAL HIGH

ARTIST AND WRITER: AL JAFFEE

A MAD LOOK AT TEACHERS

ARTIST AND WRITER: SERGIO ARAGONÉS

The Lighter Side of... School

(Part B)

ARTIST AND WRITER: DAVE BERG

It used to be that nothing short of a doctor's note detailing the symptoms of a highly contagious disease was acceptable fodder for missing a day of school. But, just as the quality of education has deteriorated, so have plausible excuses. So, to keep your ideas fresh and timely, we present you with a selection of new, improved and guaranteed to be accepted...

STUDENT EXCUSE NOTES
FOR THE 21ST CENTURY

March 5th

Dear Mr.

Please
missin
last Fri

Sincer
Ms. D

Dear Mrs. Capric,

Cory was absent last Friday because he got engrossed playing Myst and reached another level. Activities such as this are essential to helping develop Cory's hand/eye coordination. At least that's what it said in the player's manual.

Sincerely,
Cory's Parents

34 Dear Mr. Diblow,

Dear Professor,

You'll have to pardon LaRissa's absence yesterday. She was feeling the angst of being trapped in a cold, uncaring world that barely acknowledges her existence.

Best Wishes,
Mariana Pinato

Dear Mrs. Unbe,

Please excuse Melantha's absence from English class yesterday. She had to wait for FedEx to deliver her term paper.

Thank You,
Brent Sackbut

EAR TEACHER,

NE OF MY KIDS WAS ABSENT THE OTHER DAY BECAUSE OF SOME SORT OF SICKNESS, THOUGH i FORGET WHICH KID OR WHICH SICKNESS.

DAPHNE VON CATCHKEY

---

ear M
ease
issing
onda
ncer
s. Ag

Dear Sir and/or Madam:

Dag was injured in the Junior Snowboarding Championships at The 'Bird, when he bonked hard after a really aggro carve. He's still a grom, and tends to shred.

Xtremely Yours,
Dag Sr.

ARTIST: GERRY GERSTEN   WRITER: JEFF KRUSE

BESIDES GETTING YOU AN OCCASIONAL DAY OFF FROM SCHOOL, HAVE YOU EVER REALLY THOUGHT ABOUT TEACHERS' CONFERENCES? YOU PROBABLY THINK THEY SPEND THE WHOLE DAY DISCUSSING THE DEWEY DECIMAL SYSTEM AND LEARNING THE LATEST FIRE DRILL TECHNIQUES. NOT SO! THAT'S WHY IN AN UNPRECEDENTED ACT OF INVESTIGATIVE JOURNALISM, THE USUAL GANG OF DROPOUTS AT MAD NOW RIP THE LID OFF THE TEEMING CESSPOOL, STRIP BARE THE SEAMY UNDERBELLY AND SHED WARM, NURTURING SUNLIGHT ON

WHAT REALLY GOES ON AT THOSE TEACHERS' CONFERENCES!

ARTIST AND WRITER: JOHN CALDWELL

NOTICE HOW THE HIGH WAISTLINE WORKS WITH THE GIRDLE TO ENHANCE THE OVERALL PLAID EFFECT...

They hold fashion seminars.

They get together to coordinate pop quizzes for maximum student stress.

MY NAME IS ROY PETRIE....OR, AS THE KIDS CALL ME, "PEA-BRAIN PETRIE"....

HELLO, ROY!

They join in support groups to help them better cope with hurtful nicknames.

They attend student communications workshops.

They gather for their semi-annual reading of confiscated notes.

They employ role playing seminars to perfect their Good Hall Monitor/Bad Hall Monitor techniques.

The Lighter Side of... School

(Part III)

ARTIST AND WRITER: DAVE BERG

If you're a typical student, we know you just love school and can't wait to jump out of bed in the morning and get to class! Well, even though you may not have noticed, schools aren't as perfect as you think–they're full of crises (pronounced "cry-sees," look it up)! To prove our point, we scoured and combed our nation's newspapers, which resulted in much cleaner and better-groomed newspapers! We also found these articles explaining...

MODERN-DAY CRISES IN OUR PUBLIC SCHOOLS

DUNCE

    ARTIST: BOB CLARKE   **WRITER: DENNIS SNEE**

UNCHEWED PENCIL SHORTAGE ACUTE

DENVER, Colo. (UPI) — Finding a No. 2 pencil without teeth marks is now next to impossible, according to Lee Farbleberry, president of the Denver Board of education, and the situation will get worse before it gets better.

Although predictions of an unchewed writing instrument shortage were first made several years ago, nothing was done to turn the tide and the situation is now out of control.

"It disgusts me that students can deface school property so casually and not even seem concerned about it," teacher Laureen Eichberger told reporters.

The sharp increase in pencil chewing has been attributed to greater tension among young people, especially among students who now face more intense competition for top grades that can lead to college admissions.

"Yeah, I chew pencils," admitted sixth grader Amy Boswick. "But it's the American way, isn't it? I know my parents gnawed a few in their day, and if not for pencils I'd be chewing my nails, or getting an ulcer!"

The practice of sinking one's teeth into a fresh, new pencil is probably as old as the American educational system, but it is the sudden upturn in the

(cont. on page 15)

Thing of the Past? An Unchewed #2...

OLD CHEWING GUM ACCUMULATION RENDERS SCHOOL DESKS OBSOLETE

ST. LOUIS, Mo. (AP) — "The amount of old gum stuck under most school desks has finally made it impossible for the average student to sit at them!"

With this statement, school board president Stanley Sachs disclosed publicly what many have feared privately; that the build-up of gum wads under school district desks has made them unusable.

"They're like stalactites under there," said 16-year-old Denise Glut. "Last week, I ruined another pair of stockings squeezing under a desk. In fact, I almost tore a gash in my leg."

Plans to remove the old gum are being formulated, but the hardness of some of the wads may require blasting, according to one school board source.

(cont. on page 12)

Perplexed student Denise Glut wonders how she can get under her desk.

FORMER ERASER CLEANER CLAIMS CHALK DUST DAMAGES

Plaintiff Binkowitz and Attorney Baskew face reporters.

ATLANTA, Ga. (UPI) — In the third such suit filed recently, high school senior Matthew Binkowitz claimed today in municipal court that his experience cleaning erasers in elementary and junior high school caused him to develop a chronic respiratory ailment.

"I used to pound things every day till my hands got tired," Binkowitz said, "but it wasn't until a year ago that I realized breathing in all that chalk dust was bad for my health."

Binkowitz's attorney, Samuel J. Baskew, said the school board was clearly negligent in allowing the hazard to exist.

"There should be a warning printed on every eraser stating that a danger to students' health exists from chalk dust inhalation. Who knows how many may have already been exposed to the risk?"

Fellow students of Binkowitz had markedly different reactions, however.

"That Binkowitz has been a brown-noser since first grade—always cleaning erasers and watering the teachers' plants. He and all the other teachers' pets deserve whatever they get!" said one student who asked to remain nameless.

Another student offered a similar comment, saying "You notice it's only them goody-two-shoes who're complaining. Those kids get all the benefits of playing up to their teachers—let 'em take the consequences!"

Litigation stemming from the suit is likely to drag on for some time, according to a

(cont. on page 21)

Two Injured in Junior High Locker Avalanche

TRENTON, N.J. (OOPS) — Finster Junior High School students Al Elam and Byron Brooks sustained minor injuries today when they opened the locker they share and a cascade of textbooks, yo-yos, notepads, Frisbees, skateboards, a radio, a lunch box, gym bags, tennis shoes, pens, pencils and 9 half-eaten sandwiches rained down on them.

"Students have been warned that the overloading of lockers can create potential avalanche dangers," said Mr. Rupert Goop, principal of the school, "but they don't always listen. What we really fear is that they may start keeping bowling balls in their lockers! Then, you'll really see some injuries!"

The accident involving Elam and Brooks was the tenth in a series of similar incidents that

(cont. on page 45)

INK POISONING EPIDEMIC SPREADS AMONG CRIBBERS

DULUTH, Minn. (PST) — "One student had the entire Gettysburg Address written on his forearm," said Mrs. Lynn Selden, Duluth Junior High School history teacher. "He passed the final exam, but he made the mistake of using indelible ink! He had to wear long-sleeved shirts the entire month of May!"

This case, according to Mrs. Selden, is only one of hundreds being discovered each week as more and more students attempt to use their unexposed skin as crib sheets. As a result, ink poisoning within the district is increasing by leaps and bounds.

"And ink poisoning is not the most serious possible side effect of this practice," says Superintendent of Schools, Myron Grover. "What worries me is that these students aren't learning anything…except how to print very compactly!

"One student had a racket going," continued Grover. "He could write test answers so

neatly on his arms that he began Xeroxing his limbs and selling copies to other students. He made a small fortune off the football team!"

Although the chances of developing ink poisoning by writing on the skin are remote, many new

(cont. on page 42)

Remember when your mom used to put a little note and a treat in with your lunch? (No? What a sad childhood you had!) From a few scribbled lines and your favorite homemade cookies, you knew that she loved you and was thinking of you. (You really missed out, kiddo.) Yep, you can tell a lot about a mom from what she packs in your lunch. But every brown paper bag tells a different tale — and not all of them are so heartwarming. So to help decipher your mother's personality type based on her midday meal selections, MAD now presents...

STRESSED-OUT WORKING MOM

Your sister's favorite gummy snacks, not yours.

Your sandwich, accidentally wrapped in Mom's first quarter marketing report.

A can of soup with house key taped to it, with directions to microwave for dinner tonight.

ARTIST: AMANDA CONNER
WRITER: RYAN PAGELOW

LUNCH-PACKING MOM
PROFILES

EMBARRASSINGLY OVERPROTECTIVE MOM

Allergy pills in separate color-coded bags.

Overly balanced meal including selections from all four food groups, keyed to an enclosed laminated copy of the FDA Food Pyramid.

Outdated cartoon lunchbox.

Kneepads and helmet for recess in schoolyard.

NEW AGE MOM

Soy milk and horrible-tasting wheat-grass drink.

Napkins recycled from 100 percent post-consumer leftist newsletters.

Each day a new ethnic dish. Today is "Japan Day" with sushi rolls (without meat, of course), an explanation card and fun facts about Japan.

Are you tired of getting Cs and Ds on your school papers? Wouldn't you rather get A+, like the kids who take the time to study do? You can! It's simple! Getting an A+ has little to do with how much you know, and a lot to do with how much baloney you can dish out to please your teacher! Confused? You won't be once you read the following genuine examples that comprise...

THE BROWNNOSER'S GUIDE TO WRITING A+ SCHOOL PAPERS

ARTIST: BOB CLARKE   WRITER: TOM KOCH

THE SURE-FIRE A+ BOOK REPORT

"The Legend of Sleepy Hollow" is a little noan piece of litterchure that might have remaned unnoan if Miss Fennery hadnt noan to assign it, theirby making it noan to all of us.

The imajry, caracter devlopment and verbs were all neat, especialy in the middle part which a lot of students skip over, but I didnt.

The ending was good too, which I read clean up to the last word noaing that Miss Fennery wouldnt have assigned us litterchure that nobody would otherwise read unless the ending was as good as the rest of it.

THE SURE-FIRE A+ ENGLISH COMPOSITION

I spent my summer vacasion at my Mom's brother who lives near Peoria's farm, where I wandered (as Wordsworth so apply put it) "lonely as a cloud that floats on high o'er vales and hills."

I thaught at the time that I never would have known how I was wandering if Miss Neebler hadn't braudened my mind last semesser by exposing me to Wordsworth.

I also helped my Mom's brother with the pigs, but I liked thinking about Wordsworth better, which makes me glad to be back at school taking English III because Miss Neebler may expose me to Wordsworth again this semesser.

As my Christmas projeck for extra credit, I and Wanda Schimmer decorated the Teachers Lounge for Christmas. Wanda did it mostly to get a good grade for the semester which is why she told everybody she was doing it. I didnt tell nobody excepting my folks and some good friends and now in this report. Mostly I did it because I feel overcome by niceness at Christmas time.

I put all the colored jelly beans and cookies with sprinkles under the tree as my part of the projeck Wanda only hung isickles on the bottom branches as her part which is why it's not my fault that there werent enough isicles.

Sparked by Faculty Advisor Merle Badwey's rousing words of encouragement, our Blue & Gold basketeers upset the Nixon High Polecats last Friday, 71-67. Later, in the victorious dressing room, Mr. Badwey told your reporter that he felt the pre-game pep talk was his best of the year, and had been modeled after Napolean's speech to the French Army in 1814.

Mr. Badwey was an all-state debater at South Central in his undergrad days, and proved Friday that teaching without notes has kept him in shape. Another good performer against Nixon High was Slats Gander who scored 43 points.

Whether you live in a small town or a large metropolis, nothing is more important that how good your high school's football team is. A state champion means bragging rights for life. But a loser means merciless teasing that can *scar you* for life! So how do you protect yourself? Take the time to check out your school's pigskin players — and have that transfer application ready if you spot any of the...

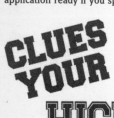

CLUES YOUR HIGH SCHOOL'S FOOTBALL TEAM REALLY STINKS

ARTIST AND WRITER: JOHN CALDWELL

Your starting middle linebacker misses four games following injuries sustained while being stuffed into a locker by the debate team.

Instead of studying game films of your next opponent, your coach runs a 45-minute continuous loop of Charlie Brown trying to kick a football.

Rather than hand signals, plays are sent in via a complicated system of Post-it notes.

By midway through the second quarter it becomes painfully obvious that the coach's headset is tuned to Latin dance music.

The team's playbook is 300 pages long and 239 of them diagram "plays to call on 3rd and 49."

A crew from America's Funniest Home Videos shows up at every game.

By the third quarter, the opposing team's mascot is playing fullback and putting up Heisman numbers.

By our judgment, watching other drivers pick their nose has dropped to #2 on the list of the most annoying things you can see while waiting at a red light! What's #1? It's those awful bumper stickers announcing some-one's son/daughter/whatever has been named Honor Student at Such-And-Such School! Who gives a flying rat's patootie, especially since none of our readers are honor students anyway? For them and their proud par-ents, we suggest they polish up the bumper on the 'ol Dodge Neon and slap on a few of these…

ARTIST: PAUL COKER   WRITER: JEFF KRUSE

MONROE &...

It's time to join your newest, bestest buddy Monroe on a painful, torture-filled journey!

"Rise and shine, Monroe! It's time to get you some new clothes at the mall!"

"KEEP OUT You"

"The... MALL?!?"

"Let's start with some dungarees! You like those, right?"

GAL

"Look! A clearance on acid washed! We'll get them really long and then let the hem down as you get taller! That way, they'll last for a few years!"

FINAL CLEARANC

GeRaLDo'S CRAZY "80's DISCO ACID WASHED JEAN'S $14⁹⁹

EAT ME THE STUFFED POTATO

"Monroe, you haven't touched your stuffed potato since we sat — Say, don't you go to school with those girls? YOO HOO! HI, GIRLS! Say hello, honey!"

T.J. & BOBS

ARTIST: BILL WRAY   WRITER: ANTHONY BARBIERI

THE SCHOOL CLOTHES

The
Lighter
Side of...
School
(Part IA)

ARTIST AND WRITER: DAVE BERG

ONE TUESDAY AFTERNOON AFTER SCHOOL

ARTIST AND WRITER: DON MARTIN